TRANS FORMERS

ADVENTURES
VOLUME 2

SCRIPT SIMON FURMAN

ARTISTS BOO < STAZ JOHNSON < SIMON WILLIAMS < JEREMY TIONGSON
FABIO MAKOTO ONO < PAUL RIDGON < MARCELO MATERE

TRANS FORMERS ADVENTURES

VOLUME 2

ISBN: 9781845768379

Published by Titan Books, a division of Titan
Publishing Group Ltd., 144 Southwark Street, London, SE1 0UP.

Printed in Spain.

First published: August 2008
2 4 6 8 10 9 5 3 1

What did you think of this book? We love to hear from our
readers. Please email us at readerfeedback@titanemail.com,
or write to us at the above address.

www.titanbooks.com

WHO ARE THEY?

They're a race of sentient robots with the power to alter their physical forms.

WHERE ARE THEY FROM?

Cybertron – a planet of living metal. Its power source is the Allspark – a giant cube generating unimaginable amounts of energy.

IS CYBERTRON A PLACE I'D LIKE TO VISIT?

If you need scrap metal! Cybertron, once a place of great beauty, is now a badly damaged hulk, ravaged by the endless war between the Autobots and the Decepticons.

THE WHO AND THE WHAT?

The Autobots and the Decepticons – bottom line: the good guys and the bad guys. The Autobots believe in honour and justice, steered by the guiding light and awesome presence of Optimus Prime. The Decepticons have been twisted by the tyrannical leadership of Megatron, whose desire for the Allspark has driven him over the edge of sanity. Their war has left their home planet in ruins.

SO WHERE DOES THIS LEAVE THINGS?

The war is over... for now. With Megatron apparently defeated and the Allspark gone, the Decepticons are in disarray. But the ever-ambitious Starscream has yet to make his grab for power...

TRANSFORMERS 101

SCRIPT SIMON FURMAN ⬡ **ARTWORK** BOO ⬡ **COLOURS** ROBIN SMITH ⬡ **LETTERING** JIMMY BETANCOURT/COMICRAFT

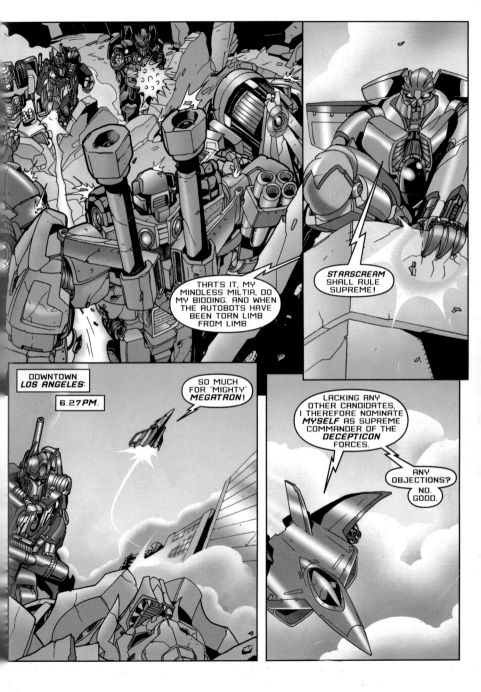

NOW ALL I NEED... ARE SOME *ACTUAL* FORCES TO COMMAND!

THABOOM

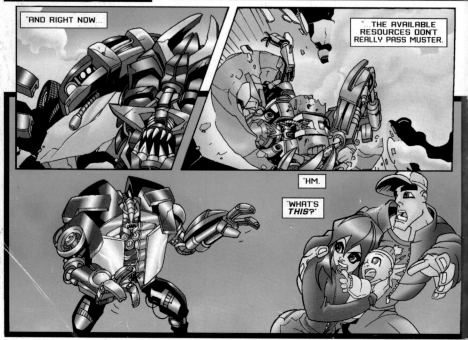

"AND RIGHT NOW...

"...THE AVAILABLE RESOURCES DON'T REALLY PASS MUSTER.

"HM.

"WHAT'S *THIS*?"

7

9

11

SKAWT

FTUM!

ALLSPARK ENERGY?

HUMAN MECHANICAL DEVICES, EXPOSED TO ITS CORRUPTED INFLUENCE. *SOMEONE* GOT TO THEM.

WHO?

"...IS IT *TRULY* OVER?"

I THINK I *MIGHT* BE ABLE TO HAZARD A GUESS. WHAT I WANT TO KNOW IS...

FRENZY

INTRODUCTION

In his chosen field of espionage and infiltration, Frenzy has few (if any) peers. There's almost nowhere he can't go and no secret he can't extract. And what's more, Frenzy goes about his work with enthusiasm, utterly contemptuous of the so-called security measures designed to keep him out. But while Frenzy is largely renowned for covert operations, he's equally adept at sowing chaos and inflicting damage (on a scale that his small size might not readily suggest). In fact, this aspect of Frenzy's work really sparks his ignition. He delights in carnage. His single-minded zeal when it comes to inflicting pain is legend, and once set on a course of action he can neither be reasoned nor bargained with.

HISTORY

BEHIND ENEMY LINES

In the early stages of Megatron's campaign to subjugate Cybertron, Frenzy was a key player. While the first shots were being fired, Frenzy was already hard at work behind the scenes, amassing data on the defensive capabilities of Optimus Prime's forces, and intercepting coded Autobot communications. Frenzy operated almost entirely behind enemy lines, alone and isolated from the main Decepticon force. But where others might have eventually crumbled under the pressure of isolation, Frenzy thrived. And if he got to kill an unwary Autobot or two along the way, so much the better! Frenzy quickly became utterly indispensable to Megatron.

ROBOT MODE

- Frenzy's de-centralised nervous system makes him very hard to kill. He can continue to function even if badly damaged.

- Frenzy has a lethal array of offensive options, including a sonic shockwave/screech (which can crash an entire neural net), a laser cutter and his chest-mounted disc-slinger, which launches circular discs with razor sharp barbs, one at a time or in a rapid-fire sequence.

- These so-called 'discs of death' can slice through even the toughest armour, and spin at a staggering 500 RPM.

ALT. MODE

- On Earth, as on Cybertron, Frenzy found numerous appliances and gadgets of a size that suited his multi-transforming, invasive abilities.

- He can be anything from a boom box to a PDA to a mobile phone, and thus disguised, go anywhere unnoticed.

- Frenzy changes his alt. form frequently, making him very hard to locate or keep track of.

- Frenzy is nimble and multi-jointed, with a hyper-reactive trans-scanning /reformatting processor, enabling him to transform at speed.

SCALE RELATION CHART

— 3'

FRENZY

BONECRUSHER

INTRODUCTION

Where some Decepticons run on greed or ambition or just the sheer love of carnage, Bonecrusher runs on pure, unadulterated hate. He hates everything and everyone, friend or foe. He even hates himself, despising his hunched, misshapen robot form, which he believes is a reflection of his inner ugliness and an outward representation of his twisted mind. Naturally, it's Bonecrusher's enemies who get the full impact – literally – of all this self-loathing and bitterness, as he takes out (vents!) his anger and frustration on them in one brutal, bruising assault after another. Mean, vicious and a master of fighting dirty, Bonecrusher is utterly, slavishly dedicated to the art of war and strikes while others are still formulating their strategy.

VEHICLE MODE

- In vehicle mode (currently a modified Buffalo MPCV mine clearer), Bonecrusher sows random collateral damage with his claw arm, creating multiple distractions that can cause his prey to take their eye off him at the critical moment.

- The sheer thunderous mass of him allows Bonecrusher to crash right through heavily fortified barricades and siege defences with little or no damage to himself.

- Bonecrusher's claws are loaded with sensitive probes which, when inserted in the ground, can detect the presence of buried explosive devices and disarm/remove them.

HISTORY

TIGHTLY WOUND

On Cybertron, Bonecrusher was often frustrated by the lack of fighting afforded him by his role as senior battlefield tactician. Often, rather than actually gutting some poor unfortunate Autobot who stood between him and his objective, Bonecrusher was consigned to calling the shots, structuring the overall tactical offensive from a rearguard position. This just increased his level of frustration, to the point where he'd take on anyone — in the heat of battle, Bonecrusher would go one-on-one with Optimus Prime without a second thought! Megatron is only too happy to exploit this intensity...

WEAPONS MODE

- Bonecrusher's claw arm is multi-functional. The carbon-tungsten tips can tear through armour plating, stone and even energy forcefields.

- In its intact configuration, the claw (on a 360 degree extendable crane arm) can cause mayhem left, right and centre, or it can separate into two independent units, protecting either flank.

- The claw also has a rotating joint, and can spin at high speed. In a pursuit situation the extra distance enabled by the extension of the crane arm can be decisive.

SCALE RELATION CHART

ROBOT MODE

- Bonecrusher is deceptively fast, his visibly ungainly form actually a clever design sleight of hand.

- In robot mode, Bonecrusher can accelerate from standing to an attack speed of 50 mph in just two seconds, disguised roller features (with a gravity null field) in his feet enabling him to glide across flat ground effortlessly.

- Built from reinforced layers of a cobalt/tungsten amalgam, Bonecrusher can soak up lots of close quarters punishment while striking back with pile-driving force.

- His knowledge of how and where to hit to do the most damage is legendary.

BONECRUSHER

CHARACTER PROFILE

SCRIPT SIMON FURMAN ● ARTWORK STAZ JOHNSON ● COLOURS KRIS CARTER ● LETTERING JIMMY BETANCOURT/COMICRAFT

"... A *SLAVE* TO THE WILL OF *SCORPONOK*!"

EARLIER:

AL UDEID AIR BASE, QATAR...

WHERE'S *LENNOX*?

REASSIGNED.

I'M *CAPTAIN CARTWRIGHT*. YOU'RE *IRONHIDE*, RIGHT?

RIIIGHT. WHY WASN'T I TOLD OF THIS CHANGE OF PLAN? AS I UNDERSTOOD IT, THIS WAS *PERSONAL*.

IT WAS. IT *IS*. BUT CAPTAIN LENNOX IS A GOOD SOLDIER. HE FOLLOWS ORDERS, EVEN IF RIGHT NOW THEY TAKE HIM SOMEWHERE *OTHER* THAN HERE.

WE'RE FILLING IN.

YOU'VE BEEN BRIEFED?

UM-HM. BELIEVE ME, WE KNOW EVERYTHING THERE IS TO KNOW ABOUT THE *TARGET*... AND *YOU*.

FIRST, THOUGH, LET ME INTRODUCE YOU TO THE TEAM.

WARRANT OFFICER *MARCUS HOLT*...

'KAY.

MASTER SERGEANT *CARLOS JIMENEZ*...

HEY.

WEAPONS SERGEANT *DARIUS GALE*...

YO.

SERGEANT FIRST CLASS *WILLIAM OATES*, OUR MEDIC...

AN HONEST-TO-GOSH A-LI-EN. NOW I CAN DIE HAPPY!

OPERATIONS SERGEANT *JIM MOON*...

THIS IS THE FORMAL PAPERWORK.

NOW, BEFORE WE GO *HUNTING*, PERHAPS YOU CAN SHOW US SOME CREDENTIALS.

CREDENTIALS? HM...

...HOW'S *THIS*?

I GUESS THAT'LL DO.

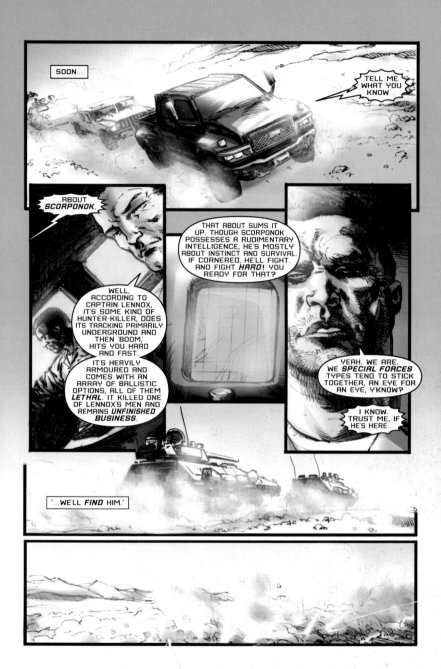

SOON...

TELL ME WHAT YOU KNOW...

...ABOUT *SCORPONOK*.

THAT ABOUT SUMS IT UP. THOUGH SCORPONOK POSSESSES A RUDIMENTARY INTELLIGENCE, HE'S MOSTLY ABOUT INSTINCT AND SURVIVAL. IF CORNERED, HE'LL FIGHT. AND FIGHT *HARD*! YOU READY FOR THAT?

WELL, ACCORDING TO CAPTAIN LENNOX, IT'S SOME KIND OF HUNTER-KILLER, DOES ITS TRACKING PRIMARILY UNDERGROUND AND THEN 'BOOM,' HITS YOU HARD AND FAST.

IT'S HEAVILY ARMOURED AND COMES WITH AN ARRAY OF BALLISTIC OPTIONS, ALL OF THEM *LETHAL*. IT KILLED ONE OF LENNOX'S MEN AND REMAINS *UNFINISHED BUSINESS*.

YEAH. WE ARE. WE *SPECIAL FORCES* TYPES TEND TO STICK TOGETHER, AN EYE FOR AN EYE, Y'KNOW?

I KNOW. TRUST ME, IF HE'S HERE...

"...WE'LL *FIND* HIM."

A HAPPY ENDING.

SOMEWHERE, I'M SURE, THERE *IS* ONE.

IN SOME *OTHER* REALITY, MAYBE JUST A SKIPPED PUMP-BEAT FROM OUR OWN, SAM'S DESPERATE GAMBIT SUCCEEDED...

...AND MEGATRON WAS CONSUMED BY THE APOCALYPTIC *ALL SPARK* ENERGIES HE SOUGHT TO COMMAND.

AND WE...

...LIVED *HAPPILY EVER AFTER* ON OUR NEW HOME – EARTH.

SOMEWHERE...

SCRIPT SIMON FURMAN ● ARTWORK SIMON WILLIAMS ● INKS LEE BRADLEY ● COLOURS KRIS CARTER
LETTERING JIMMY BETANCOURT/COMICRAFT

WAIT!

I SEE IT.

THIS IS MADNESS! CAN WE *REALLY* GET ALL THE WAY IN WITHOUT BEING DETECTED?

BUMBLEBEE?

I THINK SO, *MIKAELA*. I... *HOPE* SO.

WE *HAVE* TO FIND HIM. WHATEVER ELSE WE DO TONIGHT, WHATEVER ELSE WE ACHIEVE, WITHOUT *HIM*...

...IT'LL ALL BE FOR NOTHING.

I JUST WISH I HADN'T LET YOU TALK ME INTO BRINGING YOU ALONG. IF SOMETHING SHOULD HAPPEN TO YOU, I —

LISTEN! DON'T YOU DARE START TRYING TO WRAP ME IN COTTON WOOL! I'VE PROVED MYSELF IN THE FIELD ENOUGH TIMES ALREADY. AND ANYWAY...

...THIS IS FOR *SAM*!

ELSEWHERE...

SOON NOW, *SOON*...

THE WORLD IN WHICH THOSE FEW REMAINING AUTOBOTS STILL SCURRY AND HIDE IS BECOMING *EVER* SMALLER. WE STAND ON THE BRINK OF A GLORIOUS NEW ERA OF *DECEPTICON* SUPREMACY.

DROPKICK...

THE PLANET ITSELF HAS FINALLY, IRREVOCABLY YIELDED TO THE ALL SPARK'S INFLUENCE, ORGANIC CHAOS GIVING WAY TO MACHINE-TOOLED ORDER. *CYBERTRON*...

...SHALL BE REBORN!

YES, LORD MEGATRON?

SIGNAL *DREADWING* AND *STARSCREAM*. EARTH'S REMAINING FREE NATIONS HAVE MADE CLEAR THEIR INTENT TO RAIN NUCLEAR FIRE UPON US IF WE NOT CEDE OUR NEW TERRITORY. I INTEND...

...TO GIVE THEM OUR *ANSWER!*

THE MOON...

STRANGE. IT LOOKS SO *PEACEFUL* FROM HERE.

WELL, IT'S GOING TO GET REAL *HOT* REAL SOON, *ARCEE*... UNLESS *WE* DO SOMETHING ABOUT IT!

EH. THE SIX OF US VERSUS A WHOLE LEGION OF DECEPTICONS — HOW'S THAT WORK AGAIN?

THE ELEMENT OF SURPRISE, *LONGARM*, IT'S WHAT WE GOT. IT'S ALL WE GOT.

SO WHEN DO WE GO?

SOON AS WE HEAR FROM *IRONHIDE* AND BUMBLEBEE. ANY SOONER...

...AND WE MIGHT AS WELL SHOOT OURSELVES HERE AND BE DONE WITH IT!

...SHOOT OURSELVES HERE AND BE DONE WITH IT!

HM.

STARSCREAM...

...YOU'RE *UP!*

"THAT'S IT."

OUR WAY *IN*.

YOU KNOW WHAT TO DO.

SURE. SOON AS YOU ENGAGE TALL DARK AND UGLY THERE, I DO MY LEVEL BEST TO DEFUSE THE AUTOMATIC BLAST-CAP ASSEMBLY BEFORE IT DETONATES AND *SEALS* THE TUNNEL ENTRANCE.

THAT'S ABOUT IT. GOOD LUCK!

YEAH...

...YOU TOO!

OKAY, *SWINDLE*...

KERLANNG

TEN SECONDS...

...FROM INITIAL SECURE-PERIMETER BREACH TO DETONATION.

TEN SECONDS...

...TO ISOLATE THE THERMONIC CHARGE AND POWER UP A FOCUSED E.M.P PULSE.

THREE, TWO, ONE...

DANGER!

BOOM!

PHEW! THAT WAS TOO—

KDRUNCH

CLOSE!

OOPS. MY BAD.

LET'S *GO*. THE CLOCK IS RUNNING...

"...AND THERE'S A *LOT* OF TUNNEL BETWEEN US AND *THE OBJECTIVE*."

THERE.

RIGHT. ONE WAY OR ANOTHER...

...IT'S *SHOWTIME!*

NOW ALL WE HAVE TO DO IS *FIND* HIM AND –

OH! OH NO.

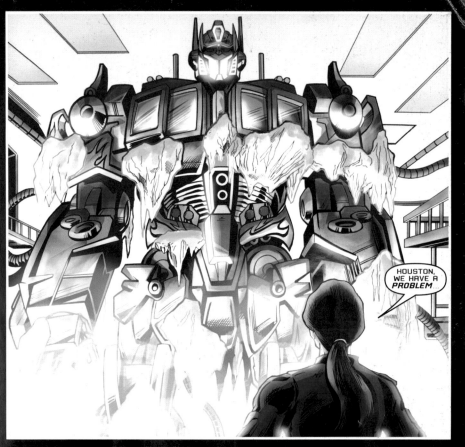

HOUSTON, WE HAVE A *PROBLEM*...

NEARBY...

...TWO *INTRUDERS* — ONE AUTOBOT, ONE HUMAN!

HM. STARSCREAM, DREADWING — PROCEED TO THE *STRIKE ZONE*. THIS IS SOMETHING...

...I'M INCLINED TO DEAL WITH *PERSONALLY*!

COME OUT, AUTOBOT!

THERE'S *NOWHERE* TO HIDE!

SKRAKT

SKRAKT

TWILIGHT'S LAST GLEAMING

PART: 2

SCRIPT SIMON FURMAN ● ARTWORK JEREMY TIONGSON ● COLOURS JASON CARDY ● LETTERING JIMMY BETANCOURT/COMICRAFT

PARIS:

ANY WORD?

NOTHING. **TWO** DEADLINES HAVE NOW PASSED AND STILL NO DIRECT COMMUNICATION FROM THE ALIENS.

NONE.

THEN WE HAVE NO CHOICE.

DIPLOMACY HAS FAILED. THREATS HAVE FAILED. CONVENTIONAL WEAPONS HAVE BEEN REPULSED.

ONLY THE **NUCLEAR** OPTION REMAINS.

AS WE **RUSSIANS** HAVE BEEN SAYING FOR **WEEKS** NOW.

SO BE IT...

SKTZAK

THE BAY OF BISCAY:

WHOMF!

STARSCREAM, THIS IS *DREADWING*. WHAT'S YOUR STATUS?

THWOM!

THE HUMANS HAVE AN EXPRESSION FOR IT: LIKE SHOOTING FISH IN A BARREL!

GOOD. AM PROCEEDING TO PRIMARY TARGET.

TWELVE MILES WEST OF SAVANNAH, GEORGIA:

SPEED LIMIT 45

"HERE THEY COME."

READY?

READY.

WAIT FOR IT, *WAIT* FOR IT...

NOW!

FDUMM

CHKRRNCH

CLASSIFICATION: AUTOBOT. IDENTIFYING... *IRONHIDE. RATCHET.*

TERMINATE IMMEDIATELY.

45

...IS DESTROY *THAT*.

THE MOON:

NOTHING.

NOT A WORD FROM EITHER IRONHIDE *OR* BUMBLEBEE.

THIS WAITIN' IS DRIVIN' ME *NUTS*. DON'T KNOW ABOUT THE REST OF YOU, BUT I'M *SPOILIN'* FOR A FIGHT!

AS IT HAPPENS, THAT...

...CAN BE *ARRANGED!*

TRANSFORMERS
TWILIGHT'S LAST GLEAMING

PART
THREE

THE MOON:

HA! IF I'D KNOWN THIS WAS THE SUM TOTAL OF THE **AUTOBOT** COUNTER-OFFENSIVE... ...I'D HAVE SENT **DRONES!**

MOVE!

THEY'VE **FOUND** US.

VTUMM! VTUMM!

SO MUCH FOR THE ELEMENT OF SURPRISE!

WRITTEN BY SIMON FURMAN
ART FABIO MAKOTO ONO
COLOURS RYAN BUTTON
LETTERS JIMMY
   BETANCOURT/COMICRAFT

SKRATOOOM

I COULD TAKE YOU ALL DOWN, WITHOUT SO MUCH AS STRAINING A DIODE. BUT, AS IT HAPPENS...

...I'VE GOT MYSELF SOME SUB-SURFACE SUPPORT!

ZzRAAKT

SCORPONOK!

THIS IS GOING FROM BAD TO WORSE.

AND IF THEY KNOW WE'RE HERE, IT SUGGESTS THE MAIN MISSION IS BLOWN. BUMBLEBEE, IRONHIDE, RATCHET... CHANCES ARE THEY'RE ALREADY DEAD.

MAYBE, MAYBE NOT. WHATEVER THE CASE, WE GOT NOTHIN' TO LEFT TO LOSE, RIGHT?

SO WHAT SAY WE TAKE THIS BATTLE RIGHT TO THE 'CONS DOOR –

– AN' KICK IT IN!

CHUNGHT

I'LL MAKE THIS *QUICK*...

FLANNNG

KTITCH

OH, AND DON'T WASTE YOUR LAST PRECIOUS MOMENTS OF CAPACITOR SPACE ON THE HUMAN. HE... SHE... IT...

"... IS *ALREADY* DEAD."

WH-WH-WH

FUNNY. BUT SEE, I'M NOT JUST UGLY. I'M MEAN WITH IT!
IRONHIDE — BACK OFF! YOU'RE NO MATCH FOR HIM IN YOUR PROTO-FORM. ATTITUDE...
... WILL ONLY GET YOU SO FAR!
TUNNK
WHEREAS THE METALS AND MINERALS IN THIS ORE...
... WILL GET YOU ARMOUR!

UHH-*UH!*

CLUMSY...

...SLOW.

SOON TO BE...

HHH-HHH...

...*EXTINCT!*

VAAARK

UNHT!

CAME HERE TO FREE *OPTIMUS PRIME*. BOO-HOO — FAILED. *FRENZY* WINS.

NEVER MIND.

SOON BE *COLD* AND *DEAD*.

"...IT'S A CASE OF **WHO** BLINKS FIRST!"

ZREEK

I THOUGHT YOUR VOCAL INTERFACE HAD REPAIRED ITSELF, AUTOBOT. AT LEAST HAVE THE DECENCY...

WHKAP!

...TO *SCREAM!*

ONE PLAINTIVE, BROKEN SOB, A CRY FOR MERCY AND I'LL *CONSIDER* ENDING THIS TORMENT. BELIEVE ME...

ZREEK!

I COULD DO THIS *ALL NIGHT!*

I·IS...

THAT ALL YOU *GOT?*

SO WE CAME TO LEND A HAND.

MUCH APPRECIATED. NOT TO SOUND UNGRATEFUL, BUT UNLESS MIKAELA HAS ACHIEVED THE *MAIN* OBJECTIVE...

...IT'LL ALL COUNT FOR EXACTLY *NOTHING!*

SPAKT!

HUT!

TOM? ARE YOU SURE I'M HEADED IN THE RIGHT DIRECTION? THIS PLACE IS A MAZE!

YOU SHOULD BE *NEARLY* THERE...

LOOK FOR A DOOR ON YOUR RIGHT MARKED *FIRE SAFETY.*

WHAT YOU'RE AFTER IS INSIDE.

OKAY. GOT IT.

ENTER: RESPONSE: 9-1-1. AND MIKAELA...

YEAH?

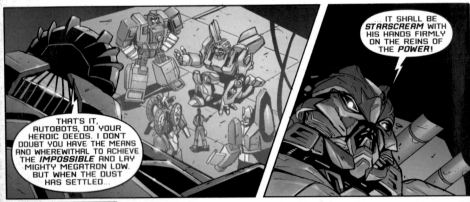

...IT SHALL BE *STARSCREAM* WITH HIS HANDS FIRMLY ON THE REINS OF THE *POWER!*

THAT'S IT, AUTOBOTS, DO YOUR HEROIC DEEDS. I DON'T DOUBT YOU HAVE THE MEANS AND WHEREWITHAL TO ACHIEVE THE *IMPOSSIBLE* AND LAY MIGHTY MEGATRON LOW. BUT WHEN THE DUST HAS SETTLED...

SAVANNAH, GEORGIA.

ALLSPARK POWER DISTRIBUTION-HUB:

"SO *NEAR*..."

...AND YET SO *FAR!*

YEH. WHATEVER SLIM CHANCE WE HAD OF HALTING THE *REFORMATTING* OF PLANET EARTH IS GONE. JUST *GONE.*

NO! I WON'T ACCEPT THAT, I *WON'T!*

FACE IT, *ARCEE* — OUR ONLY CHANCE NOW IS TO OVERLOAD THE *CORE* WITH OUR ENERGY ACCELERATOR WEAPONS...

...BUT THERE'S JUST *NO WAY THROUGH!*

THEIR WAR, OUR WORLD!
YOUR COMIC!

FREE! AWESOME ROBOT BLASTER!

TRANS FORME *ROBOTS*

LATEST NEWS!

WIN COOL T-SHIRTS! DVDS! STUFF!!

FIRESTORM!
STARSCREAM'S REVENGE!

ON SALE NOW!

SUBSCRIBE NOW!
U.K. ☎ 0844 844 3797 EIRE ☎ 01795 414 642
WWW.TITANMAGAZINES.CO.UK

...COMING SOON
TRANSFORMERS ANIMATED COMIC!

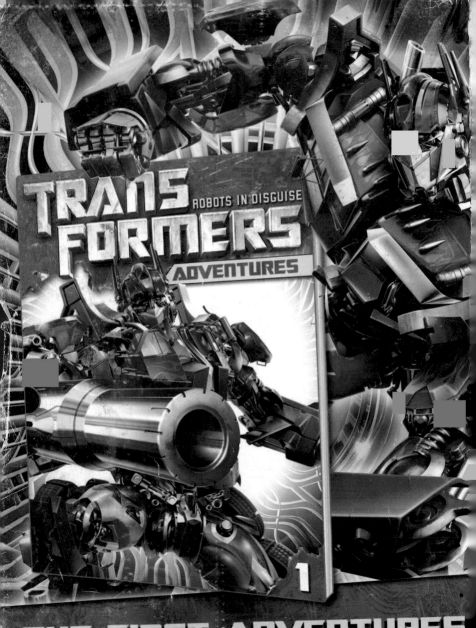